Frisk & Dexter Investigate

The case of
THE PHOTOGRAPHS

Dave & Lynn Hopwood

Kevin Mayhew

First published in 2001 by
KEVIN MAYHEW LTD
Buxhall, Stowmarket, Suffolk IP14 3BW
E-mail: info@kevinmayhewltd.com

9 8 7 6 5 4 3 2 1 0

ISBN 1 84003 830 6
Catalogue No 1500468

Edited and typeset by Elisabeth Bates
Cover designed by Amanda Smith
Illustrated by Lynn Hopwood
Printed and bound in Great Britain

'Frisk and Dexter Investigate the Case of the Photographs' is a Bible adventure where you, the reader, get involved and crack the case. At the end of each section there is a decision and you decide what should happen next by turning to the page of your choice. You begin on page 6, but after that do not read this book as you would a normal book, from cover to cover.

You will embark on the adventure with Frisk and Dexter, two time-travelling detectives. Frisk is the studious, note-taking, cautious one, Dexter the impetuous heroic adventurer.

Frisk and Dexter ran a time travel investigation agency. They were detectives who could investigate any crime from any time. They had a large brown office, with brown files and brown furniture and brown windows and brown swivel chairs. The only thing not brown was the purple phone on Dexter's desk. Whenever it rang it clattered like an old school bell, and they knew that a case from history was calling them. All they had to do was pick up the phone and they would travel back through time to the scene of the case.

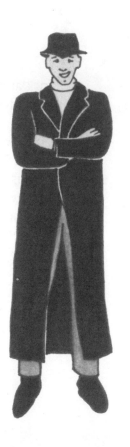

Dexter was the adventurous one. He always wore a long black coat and took plenty of risks. He had a dog called Bilko who often went with them on cases. Frisk was the more cautious one. He wore small, dark glasses and always carried a notebook and a black pencil. He'd passed all his exams at detective school with top grades.

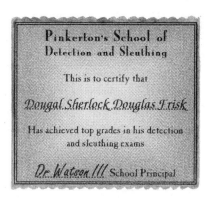

Pinkerton's School of Detection and Sleuthing

This is to certify that

Dougal Sherlock Douglas Frisk

Has achieved top grades in his detection and sleuthing exams

Dr Watson III School Principal

One Monday morning they arrived in the office to find it in a mess. Chairs were tipped over, files strewn everywhere and poor Bilko was buried underneath a mountain of discarded paper cups.

'Someone's broken in,' said Frisk.

'You bet,' said Dexter. 'Wonder what they were after.'

Frisk and Dexter searched the place as they tidied up. There were no fingerprints or footprints and there was nothing missing.

'Crazy!' said Frisk.

'You bet!' said Dexter. 'All this mess and nothing to show for it. When I get my hands on whoever did this . . .'

He stopped and pointed.

'Frisk, look!' he yelled.

The purple phone was lying on the desk, off the hook.

'That's what they were after, someone's been using the purple phone.'

'This is bad news,' said Frisk, 'very bad news. They could be anywhere in history by now.'

'And there's no way of telling where,' put in Dexter.

'Oh yes, there is,' said Frisk. 'If we dial 1471 we'll find out what date was last dialled.'

And before Frisk could move Dexter was up and dialling. He listened, frowned and then looked at Frisk.

'Wow!' he said. 'Nearly two thousand years back to AD 31.'

'Should we go after them?' asked Frisk.

'You bet,' said Dexter, and he pressed three on the phone and they found themselves hurtling back through time. (Go to page 8.)

They landed with a gasp and a thud and found themselves lying in sand. Dexter leapt up and dusted off his long black coat. Bilko appeared beside him, yapping at his heels.

'Quiet, Bilko,' said Dexter, 'I need to find out where we are.'

It was hot, it was dusty and it was midday. Frisk sat up and pulled an inflatable globe from his pocket. He blew it up and studied the result.

'I'd say we're in Palestine,' he said and he threw the globe to Dexter. Dexter headed it like a football.

Frisk pointed at the sand – a set of footprints led away to their right, towards a small desert town.

'Let's go,' said Dexter and they took up the trail.

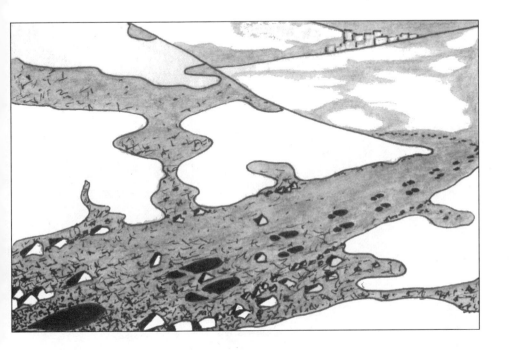

The footprints led them to the main street of the town. White houses lined either side of the dirt road. The footprints led down the deserted street and out towards a lake.

'Let's follow the prints,' said Frisk. But Dexter wasn't listening; he'd noticed a large crowd of people sitting on the hills surrounding the town.

'I'm going this way,' said Dexter and he and Bilko set off towards the hills.

Frisk wondered what to do. Should he stay on the trail and follow the prints to the lake? There might be a boat and a way across the water. That route would take him to page 10.

Or should he go with Dexter and on to page 18?

Frisk stood beside the lake. There was a single fishing boat. It looked flimsy and battered and Frisk wondered whether to try and cross the water in it. If he did cross he should take the shortest route, but which was it?

Down at his feet he could see a map drawn in the sand. He hurriedly made a copy in his notebook, but he drew the map so fast he made three mistakes.

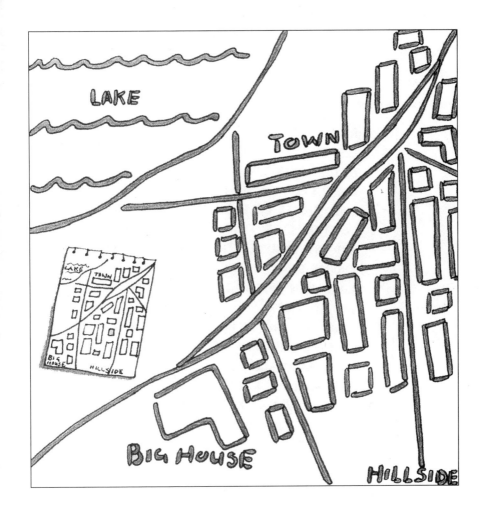

He heard a shout from across the lake and looked up. A figure was standing there calling him over. He looked at the boat. Should he go? (Go to page 14.) A set of footprints led away from the lake and towards a big, old house beside the dust road that led out of town. The place looked deserted; perhaps he should check that out? (Go to page 20.)

Frisk and Dexter pushed their way through the crowds. It wasn't easy as the place was packed with people. Men, women and children barred their way and soon the man in the green coat had disappeared.

'Drat!' said Dexter. 'Lost him.'

They stood panting at the foot of the hills.

'Hold on,' said Frisk. 'Looks like he dropped this.'

> A RICH MAN HAD A FERTILE FARM THAT PRODUCED FINE CROPS. HIS BARNS WERE FULL TO OVERFLOWING. SO HE SAID, 'I KNOW! I'LL TEAR DOWN MY BARNS AND BUILD BIGGER ONES. THEN I'LL HAVE ROOM TO STORE EVERYTHING. AND I'LL SIT BACK AND SAY TO MYSELF,"MY FRIEND YOU HAVE ENOUGH STORED AWAY FOR YEARS TO COME. NOW TAKE IT EASY! EAT, DRINK AND BE MERRY!"'
>
> BUT GOD SAID TO HIM, 'YOU FOOL! YOU WILL DIE THIS VERY NIGHT, THEN WHO WILL GET IT ALL?'
>
> A PERSON IS A FOOL TO STORE UP EARTHLY WEALTH BUT NOT TO HAVE A RICH RELATIONSHIP WITH GOD.
>
> 1 PHOTO = 1 MILLION   10 = 10 MILLION

'Looks like another one of Jesus' stories,' said Frisk.

'It is,' said Dexter, 'the parable of the rich fool. I wonder why he noted that down?'

'Perhaps he wants to get rich quick,' said Frisk.

'Yep,' agreed Dexter.

Just then Frisk felt a tap on the shoulder, he spun round and saw a bandaged figure looking like an Egyptian mummy standing there: the man was wrapped in rags from head to foot. Frisk leapt back in shock and Dexter had to catch him. Then a voice spoke and a woman stepped out from behind the bandaged man.

'Sorry to scare you,' she said, 'but we're looking for someone.'

'So are we,' said Dexter. 'Have you seen a guy in a green coat?'

The man in the rags pointed back towards the lake.

'Why's he all wrapped up like that?' asked Frisk, and he pulled out his notebook.

'He's got leprosy,' said the woman, 'so don't get too close.'

Frisk and Dexter took three steps back.

'What about you? Surely you should keep away from him,' said Dexter.

'Oh no,' said the woman, 'I've already had it.'

Frisk and Dexter looked amazed. The woman looked as healthy as they did.

'I got better,' she said, 'because I went to see Jesus. We're looking for him now so that he can help my friend here.'

Frisk pointed up the hill and they stepped back and watched as the two figures walked past them and went on up to the crowd.

'Wow! This Jesus guy must be a bit special if he can fix leprosy. That doesn't just go away on its own.'

'Come on,' said Dexter. 'Let's go check out the lake.' (Go to page 32.)

Frisk climbed into the boat and pushed off from the shore. There was only a slight breeze and the sail was ragged and torn so he had to use the single oar to paddle through the water, like a canoe. It took a long time but the figure on the other side of the lake didn't look as if he was going anywhere in a hurry.

As he approached the shore he could see that the man was a tall soldier, with huge shoulders and a rough, stern face. He was brandishing a short sword and waving it at Frisk. Frisk backed away to the rear of the boat. Was the soldier dangerous? Perhaps he should stay away? (Go to page 22.)

'Come here,' called the soldier. 'I need your help.'

Frisk couldn't work out if it was a trap or not. He cautiously began to paddle in towards land, his heart pounding in time with the splash of the oar as he rowed in. (Go to page 26.)

Frisk left the crowds behind and found himself back in the town.
He looked around for somewhere to buy food, but everywhere was
closed. He wondered if all the townspeople were up on the hill with the
crowds. As he came to a stop in the middle of the dust road that ran
through the town, his foot crunched on something and he looked
down. There were tiny bits of glass beneath his feet. That was odd –
glass like that hadn't been invented at that point in time, yet here there
were some wafer-thin glass fragments lying on the ground. He laid out
the pieces and tried to figure out what they were.

As he bent over and studied them he was suddenly hit from behind and
knocked flat. His mouth and eyes full of dirt, he sat up and spat the bits of
sand and dust out. An old woman was standing there looking a bit sheepish.

'Who hit me?' said Frisk.

'Me,' she said and she gave a nervous giggle.

Frisk looked amazed. 'What d'you mean, You?'

'Sorry, I was running so fast I couldn't stop and I saw you too late so I just ran straight into you.'

'Where's the fire?' said Frisk and when the old woman looked bewildered, he said, 'I mean what's the rush?'

'Oh, I've just never been able to do it before!'

'What?'

'Rush around! And knock people over! I used to be too ill!'

'Someone must have given you a miracle pill then,' said Frisk and he polished his front teeth on his sleeve to get the last bits of dust out.

'Oh yes, he gave me a miracle all right. He took my sickness away. I was in a really bad way and all I did was touch his coat and now I feel wonderful. It's fantastic! I've tried so many doctors and none of them could help. All I did was spend a fortune on medicines that couldn't cure me. But now, yippee! I'm better!'

And she leapt in the air, kicked her heels together and knocked Frisk backwards again.

'Ow!' said Frisk as he bashed his head against the floor.

'Oh dear! Are you hurt? I could take you to Jesus and he could fix you like he did me,' she said.

'No I'm fine,' said Frisk, 'just don't come too close to me.'

And he struggled to his feet and backed away. The woman turned and went dancing back down the street. Frisk dusted himself off and headed through the town to the lake. As he neared the water he heard a shout and looked up to see a figure waving to him across the lake. There was a boat on the shore; he wondered if he should jump in and cross over the water. (Go to page 14.) On the other hand, perhaps he should search around a little more for Dexter? (Go to page 44.)

Frisk ran after Dexter and Bilko. They were going at a fair pace so he had to run fast to keep up. As they started up the hill towards the crowds, they spotted a figure in the middle. As they got nearer they could hear him talking. He was telling a story.

'Suppose one of you goes to see a friend to borrow some bread,' the man was saying. 'It's midnight and you knock on his door. What do you think he'll do? That's right, he'll tell you to go away. So you knock again, louder this time. But he shouts back even louder, "Go away!"'

'So you knock even louder and it wakes up the neighbours, so your friend gets a bucket of bathwater and throws it over you.

'But eventually, if you don't give up, he'll get up and give you what you want. Well, sometimes it's like that when you pray. You have to keep on asking God, and not give up.'

'Who is that?' whispered Frisk as he and Dexter stood on the grass watching.

'Don't you know?' said Dexter. 'That's Jesus. We must have come back in time to Galilee.'

The man started saying a prayer so Frisk pulled out his notebook and jotted it down.

'I don't get this,' said Frisk, 'why would anyone . . .'

Our Father in heaven:
May your holy name
be honoured;

may your kingdom come;

may your will be done
on earth as
it is in heaven.

Give us today
the food we need.

Forgive us the wrongs
we have done,
as we forgive
the wrongs that others
have done to us.

Do not bring us
to hard testing,
but keep us safe
from the evil one.

Suddenly there was a click and a flash from behind. Dexter spun round and caught sight of a figure in a bright-green coat running away through the crowd.

'Get him!' yelled Dexter and he sped off.

Should Frisk go too? (Go to page 12.) Or should he hang around and see if the man in the coat had left any clues behind? (Go to page 24.)

Frisk edged his way up the dusty path to the house. The garden was overgrown and the house was crumbling and broken-down. He knocked but there was no reply. He pushed at the large front door; it creaked open and he eased his way inside. The place was a shambles. Furniture was tipped over, clothes strewn everywhere. It looked worse than their office. Suddenly Frisk heard a footstep behind him; he spun round just as a figure leapt at him through the semi-darkness. A hand snaked around his throat, the two of them struggled and Frisk staggered about the room until he fell crashing to the floor in a cloud of dust.

'Let go!' yelled Frisk. 'Let go! Who are you?!'

'Who are you, more like,' said a female voice.

Frisk sat up and rubbed the dust from his eyes to see a girl standing over him, a stick in her hand. She threatened him with it.

'My name's Frisk, I'm a private detective.'

'A what? It was you who made this mess, wasn't it? You've come back to steal some more of my uncle's money.'

Frisk stood up and asked her what she meant.

'You know,' she said. 'Everyone does. My uncle was the richest man in this town. He'd saved up a fortune and was just about to retire when – bang! He died.

'Just like that. I've been living here since, but just this morning I came back to find this mess, someone had broken in. Was it you?'

'No,' said Frisk, 'but I've got a good idea who it might be.'

He bent down and pulled a green glove from the dust. On it, stitched in red thread, were the initials MM.

'I think I know who this belongs to,' he said, 'a very dangerous criminal. I bet it was him who broke into our office and for some reason he's come here.'

'Why?'

'I don't know, but you can bet he's up to no good.'

'I might have known this would happen,' said the girl. 'All my uncle ever thought about was money. And now look, he hasn't got any of it; he's just worked himself into an early grave and other people have got his riches. He always said we'd have time together when he'd retired, but now it's too late.'

Frisk wondered if he should stay and help tidy up. (Go to page 28.)

Or should he move on and continue the search? (Go to page 50.)

Frisk pulled hard on the oar and the boat began to move away from the shore. He made his way further along the lake until he spotted a second boat close to the shore. There was an old man sitting inside, fixing a big, old net. Frisk rowed up alongside.

'All on your own, old man?' Frisk asked.

The old man jumped at the sound of Frisk's voice. He turned to look, his face wrinkled and weathered from years of fishing in his boat.

'My sons are off up in the hills. They used to work with me in the boat,' he said, 'but not anymore.'

'What happened?' asked Frisk.

'We were fixing our nets a few weeks ago when a chap from Nazareth came walking by. He looked at my boys long and hard, and then he asked them to go with him. I had a funny feeling right there and then I might never catch sight of them again.'

'That's a bit sad,' said Frisk.

The old man nodded. 'Yes,' he said. 'It is. But it's better for them; fishing's a good life, but from what I've heard this chap from Nazareth is amazing. Who knows what might happen now? He'll have 'em turning the world upside-down! That's what I figure.'

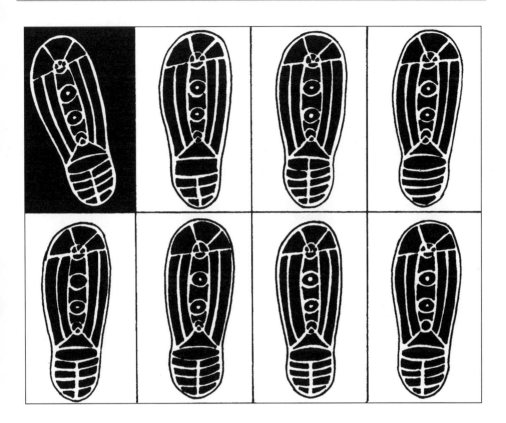

Frisk glanced inside the old man's boat and noticed a couple of muddy bootprints on the bottom.

'You given anyone a ride lately?' Frisk asked.

The old man nodded.

'A funny chap he was, wanted to get across the lake to go up into those hills outside the town.'

'What was he wearing?' asked Frisk.

'A green coat,' said the old man. 'And he was carrying something odd. Something I've never seen before. It was black and silver.'

The old man couldn't say anymore about it so Frisk thanked him and rowed on.

'What now?' he thought. Back to the town (go to page 42), or row further on down the lake? (Go to page 36.)

Frisk put his notebook away and pulled out his magnifying glass. He scrabbled about in the grass looking for clues, and as he crawled between the feet of the crowd some of them stepped on his hands. It was worth the trouble though, Frisk found this:

Just then a shadow fell over him and he looked up to see a little boy standing there.

'I've got some food,' he said.

'So?' asked Frisk and he took the bag that the boy held out to him and studied the contents through his magnifying glass.

There were five loaves and a couple of fish.
'He said he wanted some food,' said the boy.
'Who did?' asked Frisk.
'The man did,' said the boy. 'The man telling the stories.'
'Better give it to him then,' said Frisk and he handed it back, 'he's over there.'

The boy disappeared and Frisk stood up. Seeing the food had made him a bit peckish. Should he go off for a bite to eat? (Go to page 16.)

Or should he stay around and see if he could find some more clues? (Go to page 30.)

Z	A	Q	M	O	N	E	Y	F	I	S	H	I	N	G	S
H	N	B	F	G	L	T	R	F	V	C	D	A	E	W	X
Y	U	J	E	M	O	D	K	I	O	P	M	Q	A	Z	S
I	K	M	E	J	O	U	W	N	H	H	Y	T	G	X	D
O	R	L	D	A	F	S	W	O	C	E	D	C	V	F	N
M	E	J	I	U	H	N	H	I	M	Y	B	G	T	R	E
I	T	K	N	O	C	L	R	P	F	A	S	Y	F	C	I
C	A	B	G	M	I	Y	S	R	D	D	N	U	J	V	R
X	W	G	F	A	R	U	N	A	W	A	Y	S	O	N	F
M	M	Z	I	E	I	N	K	R	B	N	F	O	U	F	N
I	O	C	V	H	T	S	A	E	V	O	K	S	P	I	E
F	R	I	E	N	D	A	T	M	I	D	N	I	G	H	T
G	F	M	T	S	F	E	J	I	E	T	R	P	D	Q	W
V	E	C	H	Z	B	J	A	N	F	L	S	K	C	U	D
B	N	N	O	M	L	K	J	D	E	H	T	G	F	D	S
P	I	O	U	I	U	Y	T	P	G	R	E	T	W	Q	A
F	W	J	S	S	Y	K	E	N	C	I	X	D	I	U	R
T	W	C	A	F	M	R	O	T	L	O	R	I	I	L	E
I	H	G	N	P	B	M	A	L	T	S	O	L	H	F	O
S	O	L	D	I	E	R	S	S	E	R	V	A	N	T	S

Can you find 14 miracles and parables?

'Have you got any servants?' barked the soldier.

Frisk shook his head and climbed out of the boat.

'Well I have, and they're invaluable,' said the soldier. 'I just say jump and they jump; I say get me a drink and they do it. I say tidy my room and they do it. Just like that.' The soldier snapped his fingers and the crack of it echoed around the lake.

'Well, I don't have any,' said Frisk. 'But I am after someone. Have you seen anyone suspicious around here?'

'Nope,' said the officer. 'Now – about my servant . . .'

'Why are you going on about servants all the time?' said Frisk, getting annoyed.

'Because,' said the soldier, and he stepped forward and gripped Frisk tightly by the throat, 'my best servant is ill, very ill indeed. In fact, if I don't do something, he may die.'

'Uggh, uggh, uggh,' said Frisk.

'So I'm looking for a very important man,' said the soldier. The soldier loosed his grip on Frisk and Frisk coughed and spluttered and staggered about. Then he fell over.

'Well, if you're going for a doctor, perhaps you could get me one while you're at it,' he said.

'Of course I'm not looking for a doctor. I'm looking for Jesus.'

Suddenly Frisk forgot the pain in his throat and stared wide-eyed.

'Really?' he asked.

'Of course,' said the soldier. 'If anyone can fix my servant he can. He just has to snap his fingers and my servant will be better, just like that.' And he snapped his fingers again and the sound was like a gunshot.

'In the same way that I tell my servants to jump and they do, so he can tell bad things to go away and they do. He's got a lot of power, you know.'

'I didn't know,' said Frisk.

'Well, you do now,' said the soldier. 'Now give me your boat so I can get across the lake and find Jesus.'

And without another word the soldier leapt in the boat and pushed off from the shore, leaving Frisk stranded on the shore.

Then Dexter suddenly appeared from nowhere on the far side of the lake. Now Frisk would either have to take a long walk back round the lake (go to page 32), or he could wait and scour the shore for another boat to get back across the water (see page 48).

Frisk ploughed his way through the strewn papers and upturned furniture.

'Why is the house so broken-down?' he asked.

The girl laughed. 'My uncle wasn't very popular,' she said. 'He was quite greedy and all he ever thought about was money. He wasn't really a very nice person. When he died people came round and helped themselves to bits of the house, and now it's slowly falling down. I moved in to look after the place but I haven't been very well.'

'Oh?' said Frisk. 'What happened?'

'I died.'

Frisk nearly fell over. 'What?'

'I was really ill and I died.'

Frisk went over to her and pinched her. She yelped and jumped.

'Ow!' she shouted.

'Just checking to see if you're really alive,' said Frisk.

Suddenly the door flew open and Frisk and the girl dived for cover as a figure in a long coat stepped into the doorway, blocking out the daylight.

'Hold it right there,' said Frisk, 'I'm a trained private detective.'

'So am I,' said a familiar voice.

'Dexter!' yelled Frisk.

'You bet,' said Dexter and he stepped into the house with Bilko panting at his heels.

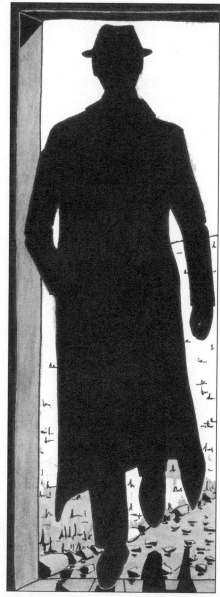

'Boy, this place is a mess,' Dexter said, looking around.

'Yes,' said Frisk, 'and look what I found.' He held up the green glove.

'That looks like Mad Mungo's glove,' said Dexter, 'come on.' He pushed his way through the house and out the back door. They stood in the garden and surveyed the hills beyond. Dexter froze and jabbed his finger at the crowds dotted on the grass.

'There he is,' said Dexter. He had top eyesight and could spot a vital clue from half a mile away. 'He's trying to hide amongst all those people up there. Look – he's wearing his bright-green coat. Let's go get him.'

Dexter sped off and Frisk started to follow. Then he glanced down and caught sight of a scrap of paper. Should he forget it and keep going? (Go to page 12.) Or should he take a closer look? He knew that it had to be some kind of clue . . . (Go to page 46.)

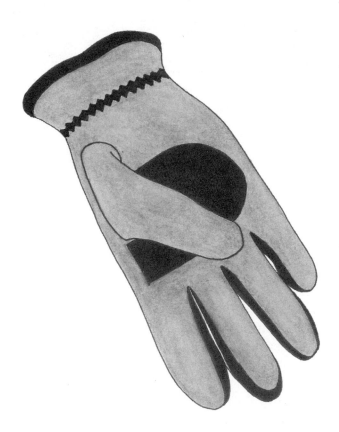

A voice called out just then telling everyone to sit down in big groups.
Frisk looked around to see what was going on, but there were so many
people it was difficult to see anything. Someone grabbed his arm and
pulled him down onto the grass. Frisk looked down to see the little boy.
    'Enjoy your lunch?' asked Frisk, pointing to the boy's empty lunch bag.
    'Haven't eaten it yet,' said the boy.
Frisk looked inside the bag. There were only a few crumbs inside.
    'Where's it gone then?' he asked.

    'I gave it to Jesus,' said the boy. 'He said he'd share it with a few
people.'
    'Well, it won't go far. How many people?'
    'Five thousand,' said the little boy and Frisk's mouth dropped open so
far his bottom lip nearly hit the grass.
    'Don't be silly!' said Frisk.
    Just then he felt a tap on his shoulder and a hand passed him a huge
pile of fish sandwiches. Frisk didn't ask where they'd come from. He
suddenly felt very hungry and all he wanted to do was eat.
    'Have you seen a man in a green coat?' asked Frisk through a mouthful
of soggy bread and fish.
    The little boy nodded.

'He's over there,' he said.

'What!' Frisk leapt up and looked over the heads of the crowd. There were people everywhere, sitting on the grass and chewing on huge fish sandwiches.

Right over at the far side Frisk could just make out a green splash of coat. Without another word he left the boy and ran off. Frisk pounded over the grass, closer and closer to the figure in green, just a few more steps and he would have him. Suddenly there was a bleating sound and a little lamb ran across his path. Frisk tripped over it, tumbled forward and went spinning across the grass.

When he sat up again the figure in green was up and running back over the hills towards the town. Should Frisk follow? (Go to page 40.)

Just then a man who looked like he was wearing a dressing gown, with a tea towel around his head, stepped out of nowhere and smiled down at him.

'Seen a little lamb?' asked the man.

Should Frisk waste precious time talking to him? (Go to page 34.)

They were soon standing together at the water's edge. The lake was calm and the water lapped softly at their feet. Bilko sniffed it and lapped at the water. It went up his nose and made him snuffle and sneeze. As they were standing looking out over the lake a man appeared and stooped at the edge. With a quick movement he pushed his hand beneath the water and scooped out a fish.

'Wow!' said Dexter. 'That was pretty cool!'

The man shrugged, prized open the fish's mouth and pulled out a coin.

'That was even better!' said Frisk.

The man threw the fish back. 'Taxes,' he muttered glumly.

'Wish I could pay my taxes with money from a fish,' said Dexter.

'Wasn't my idea,' muttered the man. 'It was Jesus who told me to come and do this. He said I'd find a coin down here in a fish's mouth.'

Dexter whistled. 'Jesus, eh?' he said. 'Now that's interesting.'

'Is it?' asked Frisk.

'You bet,' said Dexter. 'Can you introduce me to him?' he asked the man.

The man shrugged, nodded and started walking away.

'I'm going with him,' said Dexter. 'This could be a good lead. Why don't you scout around here, do some detective work and see if you can find out what's going on.'

Frisk watched them walk away then decided to check out the back streets of the town.

The houses were all deserted and everyone seemed to be out on the hills. He wondered if he should risk searching a few of the houses. Just then he heard a crash and a scuffle in a nearby doorway. He stood very still and heard the sound of fingers tapping against metal and plastic. He started to edge his way closer to the doorway when suddenly a lamb shot out from nowhere and hurtled like a stray bullet between his feet so that he tripped and fell headlong. As he hit the ground he caught his head on a stone and it knocked him out. When he came to he looked up into the face of a man who looked like he was wearing a dressing gown, with a tea towel around his head. The man looked down and smiled at him.

'Seen a little lamb?' asked the man.

Frisk didn't know whether to stay and talk . . . (go to page 34), or go and see about the crash and the scuffle he'd heard. The man may have vanished by now, but it might be worth looking around. (Go to page 52.)

'Yes, I have seen a lamb!' shouted Frisk. 'He ran right under my feet.'

'Ah! Which way did he go then?' asked the man.

'I take it you've lost him?' said Frisk, standing up and brushing the dirt off his clothes.

'I'm afraid so,' said the man. 'I'm a shepherd, see, got the best hundred sheep in the neighbourhood, but one of them ran off, so I've come looking for him!'

'And what about your other sheep . . . Where are they right now?'

The shepherd suddenly looked worried. 'Oh dear, I was so concerned about finding this one that I've left 'em all on their own . . .' Then he put on his big smile again. 'Still, they'll be all right, more important to find this lost one isn't it? Can't have him all lost on his own and getting into every kind of trouble. I couldn't bear it if anything happened to the little fella. He's one of my favourites.'

'How many favourites have you got?' asked Frisk.

'One hundred.'

'One hundred favourites? But you've only got one hundred sheep.'

The shepherd scratched his head and looked worried again. 'So I have. They must all be my favourites then, I suppose. Now then, will you come with me and help me find him?'

Should Frisk help? (Go to page 38.) Or should he try and find Dexter again? (Go to page 50.)

Frisk sailed on and the lake widened out. He was rowing hard when
suddenly he heard a clunk and a shout from over the side in the water. He
stopped rowing and looked over. There was a head bobbing in the water.

'Ow!' said the head. 'You just clobbered me with that oar!' The head
belonged to a teenager who was swimming in the lake. Frisk reached over
and pulled him into the boat.

'What are you doing swimming out here?' said Frisk.

'Going home,' said the boy. 'I ran away months ago because I couldn't
stand living at home. I was so bored and I wanted a bit of excitement.'

'Why are you going back now?' asked Frisk.

'I heard a story, about a son who took half his father's money and ran
away from home. In the story the money ran out and the boy was left
broke, so he decided to go back home and ask his dad for a job.

He thought his dad was an old miser who would give him a good telling
off when he got back, but the son was so desperate he had to go home.

When he got back his dad was really happy to see him and he threw a big party because he really loved his son.'

'So are you desperate?' asked Frisk.

The boy shook his head. 'No, just lonely; I had a wild time but now I just feel bored and empty. I want to go home.'

Frisk rowed back to the shore and the boy climbed out.

'Oi!' shouted a voice as he landed. It was Dexter. 'I've been looking for you everywhere. Come on, we need to get back to the future!'

Frisk pulled out the blue mobile and dialled their office.

'What about this case?' asked Frisk as he watched the boy walking away, back to his home in the town.

'It'll have to wait,' said Dexter, 'Bilko needs feeding.'

So that was that. Bilko barked and they went back to the future.

The search went on a lot longer than Frisk expected. They searched under bushes, in rabbit holes, behind trees and even in the pockets of nearby people. Then, as it got dark, they headed back to town and searched in the alleys, backstreets and doorways. Frisk began to lose all hope of ever seeing Dexter again, never mind the sheep.

'Look,' said Frisk, 'I've got to find my partner, Dexter . . .'

'But what about the sheep? He's in danger. Mr Duckster can look after himself, can't he?'

Frisk nodded.

'Well, my little lamb can't; you won't give up on him now, will you?'

So they searched on, and now it was really dark and they only had the light of the moon and the stars. Frisk pulled a torch from his pocket and when he switched it on the shepherd's eyes nearly popped.

'How d'you make it do that?' he asked.

'Batteries,' said Frisk, 'rechargeable ones.'

'What's butterys?' asked the shepherd.

Frisk remembered that he'd gone back two thousand years. 'Oh, not to worry,' he said. 'Just something they use where I come from.'

The shepherd shook his head, and Frisk flashed the torch around. Suddenly the man grabbed his arm.

'There!' he said. 'Just there! That's it!'

Frisk brought the torch beam around and stopped as the light settled on a little white bundle of wool. It was the lamb – he was quivering with cold and looking a little frightened too.

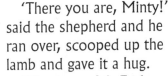

'There you are, Minty!' said the shepherd and he ran over, scooped up the lamb and gave it a hug.

'Thank you Mr Fridge, your butterys found my favourite lamb.'

'No problem,' said Frisk, 'but I'd better be off now.'

'OK then,' said the shepherd, 'hope you find Mr Duckster.'

Frisk left the shepherd with his lamb and pulled out his blue mobile phone.

He dialled the office number and before you could say 'Jumpin' Jack Flash' he found himself back in the office.

Dexter was sitting there with his feet on the desk and a camera in his hand.

'What took you so long?' he asked. 'The case is solved. I did it all on my own.'

Frisk sighed and shook his head. Oh well, at least he'd helped find the lost sheep . . .

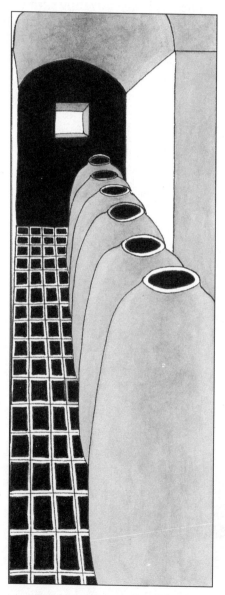

Frisk tore off back over the hills. He had to stop the green figure before it could get away. Soon he was pushing his way through the people on the hill – adults, teenagers, children – it wasn't easy fighting his way through them all. The whole town was up there now, all eating and talking excitedly. When the crowds got too thick Frisk had to stop and look for another way round.

'Want a sandwich?' asked a nearby girl.

'No,' said Frisk. 'I want to catch a man in a green coat.'

'Was he at the wedding?' asked the little girl.

'What wedding?'

'That wedding this morning, when Jesus made all the water disappear.'

'I don't know,' said Frisk. 'What happened to the water?'

'It went away, all the water vanished and there was only lots of wine. All the water jars turned into wine jars. It tasted terrible!'

'How much was there?'

'My mum said there were 180 gallons. Is that a lot?'

Frisk laughed. 'It is a lot.'

'Someone said it was the best wine they'd ever tasted, but I'm not sure.'

'And Jesus did all that?'

'Yes, he's very clever really. And I'm sure that man with the green coat was there. Hey, you can ask him. There he is!'

She pointed through the wall of people and Frisk got a glimpse of the green coat.

'Thanks!' he yelled and sped off.

Just as he drew near, the man spun round, saw Frisk and hurled a black camera case at him. The case hit Frisk on the head and he fell backwards. When he got up the man was gone. Frisk looked in the case. It was empty. He hunted around on the hill for another hour but found nothing except an old maze that someone had marked on the grass. Frisk picked one of the three starting points and followed the line – but he got it wrong and did not get to the centre.

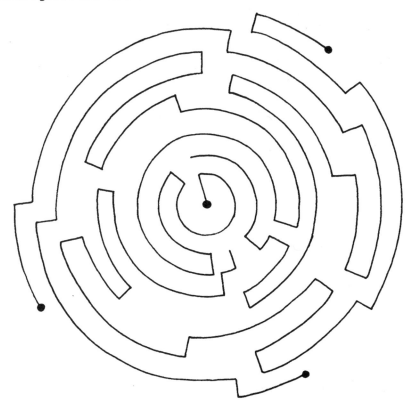

In the end he gave up, dialled the office and went wearily back to the future. Dexter and Bilko were there waiting for him, but they had not solved the case.

Frisk rowed back to the far shore and was soon standing on the edge of the town. He surveyed the scene – all was quiet. He sat down in front of a row of houses and made a few notes about the doors. He wrote them down in a strange way – can you work it out?

The first door is red, the second one is blue. The third door has a wooden handle, the fourth door is half open. The door next to the yellow one is broken. The green door is between the blue door and the yellow door. The open door has no handle and stands between the door with a shiny handle and the door with a wooden handle.

	1	2	3	4
Red				
Yellow				
Blue				
Green				
Shiny				
No handle				
Wooden				
Black				
Open				
Closed				
Broken				
Half open				

Frisk peered inside the houses through the open doorways but there was no one around and he found nothing. Then, as he stepped into a doorway, he was blinded by a flashlight exploding in his face and a figure pushed past him and out into the street. Frisk recovered his balance and took up the chase. The figure wore a long green coat and had a camera case trailing from his right shoulder. He dodged in and out of the side streets and down between the buildings but Frisk didn't give up the chase. He felt he was on the trail now. Obviously the figure in green had something to hide. As he turned a corner the camera case snagged on a tree and ripped from his shoulder. The case crashed to the ground and for a moment the figure stopped and looked back.

'Mad Mungo!' Frisk said, recognising him at once.

TOP SECRET

Mad Mungo Montgomery Marmaduke Snide
Head of the Mayhem and Muddles Crime Syndicate

Age:	Unknown
Hair:	Messy
Eyes:	Suspicious
Ears:	Waxy
Knees:	Knobbly
Suit:	Green
Gloves:	Green

Crimes: Stealing candy from babies.
Pulling the heads off jelly babies.
☐Sneezing all over his friends.
The Great Train Robbery.
Stealing the Pink Panther Diamond.

Mad Mungo Snide had been on their files for a long time. He was a very dangerous criminal and he ran a large crime syndicate.

Mungo left the camera case and ran on, afraid that Frisk might catch up. Frisk slowed as he passed the camera case. He stopped to pick it up and catch his breath.

Now Frisk had a problem.

Should he keep up the chase? Mad Mungo was just disappearing inside the garden of a big, run-down old house. (Go to page 20.)

Or should he look for Dexter and show him the camera case? (Go to page 44.)

Finding Dexter was easier said than done. Frisk had last seen him going into the hills outside the town. He searched the skyline but Dexter could be anywhere. Suddenly he heard a rustling sound in a nearby tree.

He looked up. A short stodgy man was crouching in the branches, craning his neck and looking into the distance.

'What are you doing up there?' asked Frisk.

'Looking for someone,' said the short man.

'Can you see a guy in a long black coat?' asked Frisk.

The man swung his head and surveyed the scene. 'Mmmm . . . n . . . n . . . n . . . n . . . nooo – yes!'

He pointed into the distance. 'He's over there.'

'Can I come up?' asked Frisk.

'No!' said the man. 'There isn't room.'

'Well, come down then.'

But the man shook his head. 'No way,' he said. 'Can't you see how short I am?'

Frisk couldn't, not with the man up the tree.

'I'm staying up here until the crowds clear. Then I might at last get a proper chance to talk to him.'

'Who?'

'Who d'you think? The one everyone's talking about. The man who's been helping people.'

'Well, look, in the meantime, can you see a guy in a green coat?'

'Errr . . . yes, yes, he's talking to Jesus now. You know, it's funny, but I saw him digging a hole in the street.'

'What?'

'Oh! No, hang on, he's not talking to Jesus, he's doing something else. He's pointing a black box at him and standing very still.'

'What sort of box?'

'Not very big, about the size of a large apple. Oh! That's funny. Something caught fire then, there was a flash.'

Frisk slapped a hand to his forehead. 'Of course! I know what he wants.' [Do you?]

'He probably wants to see Jesus. That's what I want,' said the man in the tree, but Frisk wasn't listening.

He was already on his way out to the hills, out to the crowds, out to solve the case . . . He reached the edge of the crowds in no time. What now? There were people everywhere. Old and young. One little boy was waving to him.

Should he push his way through the bodies and hope for the best? (Go to page 30.) As he stood wondering he remembered something the man in the tree had said. Something about the street . . . Was that a clue? Should Frisk double back and investigate? (Go to page 50.)

Frisk bent down and scooped up the paper. It had to be a clue because there was no paper like this around in the year AD 31. He opened it out.

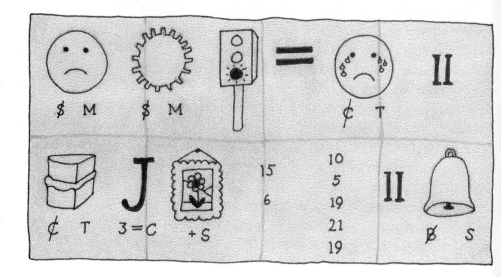

As he began to crack the code things became clearer. He realised what was going on. He had two choices now: he could go on after Dexter or he could retrace their steps and start again . . .

'What's that?' said a voice. It was the girl from the house.

'A coded message,' said Frisk. 'Listen, what was that you were saying in the house? About not being very well?'

'I died,' said the girl. 'Honest! I'm telling the truth. I was really sick and no one knew what was wrong, so I got worse and worse until I died.'

'Well you look pretty good on it,' said Frisk.

'Ah well, that's because Jesus turned up. My parents had heard that he was really good at helping sick people so they sent someone to find him. But by the time he got to our house it was too late, I was dead. He didn't give up on me though. He came into my room and the next thing I knew I woke up and there he was, standing over me and telling me to get up. Then mum and dad got me some food and I've felt fine ever since.'

'Could I meet this Jesus?' asked Frisk. 'He sounds like quite a guy.'

'Course you can . . .'

Just then the door flew open and a figure in a green coat stood panting in the doorway.

'Mungo!' yelled Frisk, his face as hard as stone, 'Mad Mungo Snide!'

'I might have known you'd come after me,' said Mungo, 'but it's too late! I'm a rich man. I've got a fortune in this case.'

He lifted up a black camera case and waved it at Frisk. Frisk lunged at him and tried to grab the case, but Mungo ducked, dived low and swung the case at Frisk's head. It knocked him out and he fell unconscious to the floor.

When he woke up, Dexter, Bilko and the girl were all leaning over him.

'You OK?' Dexter asked.

'Where's Mungo?' asked Frisk.

'Gone,' said Dexter. 'No sign of him on the hill. We could go back to the lake and check there. But it's a long shot.' (Go to page 32.)

Frisk shook his head. 'I think I'd rather go back to the drawing board and start from scratch,' he said.

He pulled his blue mobile phone from his pocket. 'If I press the redial button on here it'll take us back to the point when we first got here.' (Go to page 8.)

'What do you think, Dexter?' Frisk asked. 'What should we do?'

[What do you think?]

Frisk made his way slowly along the shore when suddenly he heard a shout. He turned and saw a smart new boat pulling in not far from him.

'Want a boat?' asked the man inside.

'I want a ride,' said Frisk.

'Well, have my boat,' said the man, and he clambered out and handed Frisk an oar.

'Where are you going?' asked Frisk, as the man began to walk away.

'Home, to sell my house.'

'But don't you want your boat back?' asked Frisk. 'It's a really nice one!'

'No, I told you, I'm going to sell my house.'

'What should I do with the boat when I get to the other side?' asked Frisk. It was a really smart craft, freshly painted, brand new and sparkling clean.

'Give it to someone else,' said the man.

Frisk suddenly got suspicious.

'You didn't steal it, did you?' he said. The man turned, glared at him, then burst out laughing.

'No,' he said, 'I worked very hard for it. In fact I worked very hard for everything I have, and guess what? I just met someone who told me to give it all away, just like that. And I'm a very rich man.'

'So what are you gonna do?'

'Well, at first I got mad, then I thought about it and do you know what? I think I'm going to do it. I'm gonna give everything away, and then I'm going to come back and tell Jesus about it.'

And with that the man turned and walked away. 'Oh, and look after the boat,' he called without looking back. 'It's worth a lot of money.'

Frisk jumped aboard and looked around. The boat was very big and not easy to handle, especially by Frisk who knew nothing about sailing. Should he row along the shore until he found another boat to help him out (go to page 22), or should he try and row across the water on his own? (Go to page 36.)

Frisk hurried back down to the main street through the town. He stood scratching his head and as he looked down he noticed a map drawn in the dirt.

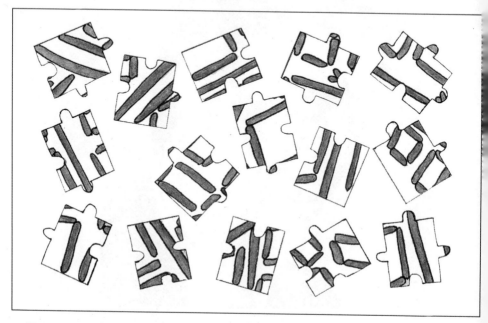

He was just bending over to study this when he heard the sound of running feet and a man ran straight into him. 'Oof!' said Frisk as he fell spinning to the floor.

'Sorry!' called the man as he ran past. 'Can't stop, I'm in a hurry.'

'Have you seen anyone in a green coat?' called Frisk.

'No, I've been going too fast to notice anyone,' called the man. Clouds of dust flew up from his heels as he continued on his way.

'What's the rush?' shouted Frisk.

'I've got to tell Jesus that he cured me,' said the man.

'Doesn't he know?' asked Frisk.

'Nope!' said the man, his voice fading away fast now. 'Me and nine of my friends all had leprosy and Jesus told us all to go and see a priest. So we went and suddenly, on the way, we were all instantly cured! So I thought I'd go back and say thanks . . .'

And his voice melted away to nothing as he ran on.

Frisk looked at the map again. Suddenly he realised it marked the place where something important was buried. He worked out where the spot was and began digging away in the dirt.

It was hard work but suddenly his hand hit something hard and black. It was a leather box.

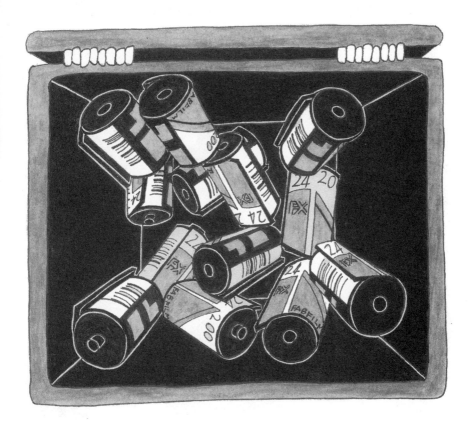

Frisk pulled it free from the dirt and dusted it off. He opened it up. Inside was a pile of used films. The box had the initials M M stitched into the top of the lid.

Frisk took the box and dialled the office on his blue mobile phone. He was going back to the future as soon as possible. He'd lost Dexter and he'd not solved the case, but he had found a vital piece of evidence and he needed to get back to the office for a rethink . . .

Frisk got to his feet and crept towards the doorway. All seemed quiet but he moved closer and peered inside. A figure in a long coat stood with his back to the doorway. A camera case was slung over his shoulder and he was hunched over in the semi-darkness.

'Gotcha!' yelled Frisk and the figure spun round.

It was Mad Mungo Snide. He held a camera in one hand and a pile of photos in the other hand.

'I'll have those,' said Frisk, and before Mungo could move he snatched the pictures from his hand and leafed through them. They were photographs of the people he'd met and the things he'd seen that day. Suddenly all the pieces began to fit together.

'If Jesus is this amazing, unique guy,' said Frisk, 'different to anyone else whoever lived, then a photograph of him and the things he has done would be worth millions, right?'

Mad Mungo nodded and clapped his hands slowly. 'Well done, Mr Frisk,' he said. 'But too late, I fear. I already have ten more pictures of his handiwork in the camera here. From the money I get for these I'll be able to fund my crime syndicate for 50 years. There'll be no stopping me now.'

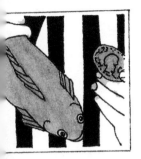

And before Frisk could stop him, Mungo lunged at him and tore Frisk's blue mobile phone from his coat pocket.

'Now,' said Mungo, backing away again, 'give me the number of your office and I'll give you your mobile phone back – once I've dialled and am on my way back to the future. If you don't give me the number then I'll smash this mobile phone of yours and you'll be stuck here for ever. There are no other telephones here – you'll never be able to dial your way back!'

Frisk thought for a minute, then he said, 'This is how I remember the number. There are six digits and they add up to 36 in total. The first number is three more than the fourth number and the fourth number is twice the second number; the second number is four more than the fifth number and the fifth is three times the sixth. The sixth number is 1.'

[Is Frisk telling the truth?]

Mungo needed all his fingers to calculate this so he slipped the mobile phone under his chin while he worked it out. Frisk took his chance then and quick as a flash he leapt at Mungo and knocked him flat.

The camera flew from his grasp and slid across the floor, spilling out a reel of film as it went. Frisk pulled out a set of handcuffs and snapped them on Mungo's wrists.

'Bad luck, Mungo,' said Frisk. 'You're going back to the future for a long time. And these pictures of yours? Well, I think we'll leave them here in Galilee where they belong.'

And Frisk punched the numbers on his mobile phone and they hurtled back to the future.

Frisk & Dexter Investigate

THE CASE
OF
THE BABY

Dave & Lynn Hopwood

ISBN 1 84003 388 6
Catalogue No 1500284

Frisk and Dexter, two time-travelling detectives, are about to embark on a mission going back in time to Bethlehem to find the baby. But this is no ordinary story book and the baby they are searching for is no ordinary baby . . .

It's up to you, the reader, to get involved and crack the case and help the detectives to find the baby. Instead of reading the book from cover to cover, you embark on the adventure with Frisk and Dexter, but you make the decision as to what happens next by turning to the page of your choice.

So, will Frisk be able to follow the clues left by Dexter and find the baby? It's in your hands, so get reading!